MOTHER NATURE TAKES A VACATION

BY LYDIA BAILEY

ILLUSTRATED BY
SYLVIE DAIGNEAULT

An Alligator Press Book
HarperCollins*PublishersLtd*

An Alligator Press Book
Consulting Editor, Dennis Lee

Published by
HarperCollins Publishers Ltd
Suite 2900, Hazelton Lanes
55 Avenue Road
Toronto, Canada M5R 3L2

92 93 94 95 96 97   First Edition   10 9 8 7 6 5 4 3 2 1

Canadian Cataloguing in Publication Data
Bailey, Lydia
Mother nature takes a vacation

ISBN 0-00-223754-7

I. Daigneault, Sylvie. II. Title.

PS8553.A55M6 1992   jC813'.54   C91-095467-4
PZ7.B35Mo 1992

For Mom
L.B.

A mon oncle Claude
S.D.

OTHER Nature was fed up. "Phooey," she said. "The people in this kingdom don't care about me. They throw garbage in my oceans, they dirty my soil, and they make my air gray and yucky. I'm going on vacation." And with that she packed up her knitting and caught a fast bird to Florida.

ROM that day on, the kingdom had a terrible time. The sun never rose, the birds never sang and, worst of all, spring never came.

Finally, in desperation, the king issued a proclamation: he offered his kingdom to anyone who could bring back Mother Nature.

 LL of the bravest people joined in the search. They looked high and they looked low. They looked east and they looked west.

They looked in forests and they looked in caves. But Mother Nature was nowhere to be found.

 N a tiny, rose-covered cottage at the edge of the forest there lived a clever girl named Sue. She had a heart of gold, and all the animals of the forest loved her. Each evening at sunset they gathered round her cottage door and she played for them on her silver flute.

NE particularly cold day the pipes in Sue's cottage froze. She had no heat and she had no water. "This is ridiculous," said Sue. "It's going to be winter forever. I've got to do something!" So she threw on her coat and her boots and stomped off to see the king.

Sue knocked loudly at the entrance to the palace, and the golden doors swung open. She marched boldly up to the king, bowed very low and said politely, but firmly, "If you please, Your Majesty, I would like to look for Mother Nature myself."

The king looked down at Sue. "You?" he sneered. "That's preposterous!"

UST then a big drift of snow pushed through the palace door. The king shivered and sneezed. "Oh, all right," he croaked crossly. "Go look for her. Surely no harm can come of it. In fact, probably nothing will come of it," he sighed, slumping despondently down into his throne.

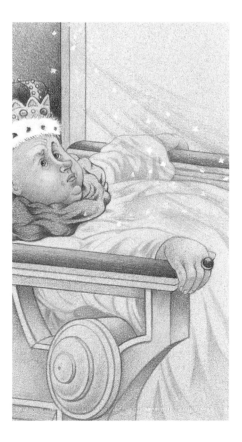

THAT night Sue packed all of her belongings into a small leather knapsack. She walked and walked and walked. She walked until she came to the end of the earth, where the sun lived. Sue found him wedged grumpily in the hollow between two hills. "Good day, Sun," said Sue. "How are you?"

"Hrrumph," he grumbled. "I'm terrible — and it's not a good day. In fact, it's not been day at all since Mother Nature disappeared. You see," he said sadly, "she used to help me get up in the morning. Without her I just can't do it."

"I can help you," said Sue. She pulled a strong piece of rope from her pack and tied it around his fat belly. She heaved and she tugged and she pulled. Slowly, the sun rose, and soon he was shining happily, way up high in the sky. "Can you tell me where Mother Nature is?" Sue called up to him.

"No," he beamed down. "But the flowers might know. Go ask them."

UE walked on and on until she came to the valley where the flowers lived. "If you please, Flowers," she inquired politely, "can you tell me where Mother Nature is?"

"Oh," sighed the flowers, swaying towards her, "we'd like to find her ourselves. She always told us which perfume to wear. Without her we don't know what to do."

"I can help you," said Sue, taking some small bottles out of her pack. Soon every flower in the valley smelled as sweet as an evening in June.

"Thank you," they whispered. "Ask the birds where Mother Nature can be found. They might know."

UE walked and walked until she came to the great, green forest where the birds lived. She could see them lined up on the branches, but she couldn't hear them — not a chirp, not a twitter.

"If you please, Birds, can you tell me where Mother Nature is?"

"Oh," tittered the birds, "we'd like to find her ourselves. She always reminded us when to start singing our morning songs. Without her we don't know what to do."

"I can help you," said Sue. She took her silver flute out of her pack and began playing softly.

Soon all the birds were cooing and cawing and chirping and whistling. "Ask the clouds," they sang. "Perhaps they can help you find Mother Nature." The birds flew up under her arms, lifted her high, high up, and dropped her down, *kerplop*, on a big, soft cloud.

F you please, Cloud, can you tell me . . ."

All at once Sue was surrounded by a crowd of clouds. "If you're looking for Mother Nature," they puffed, "we'd like to find her ourselves. She always kept us mended and stuffed. Now that she's gone we have no one to look after us."

"I can help you," said Sue. She took a pillow from her pack, shook the feathers from it, and went to work mending and stuffing. Soon each cloud was fluffy and plump and quite content.

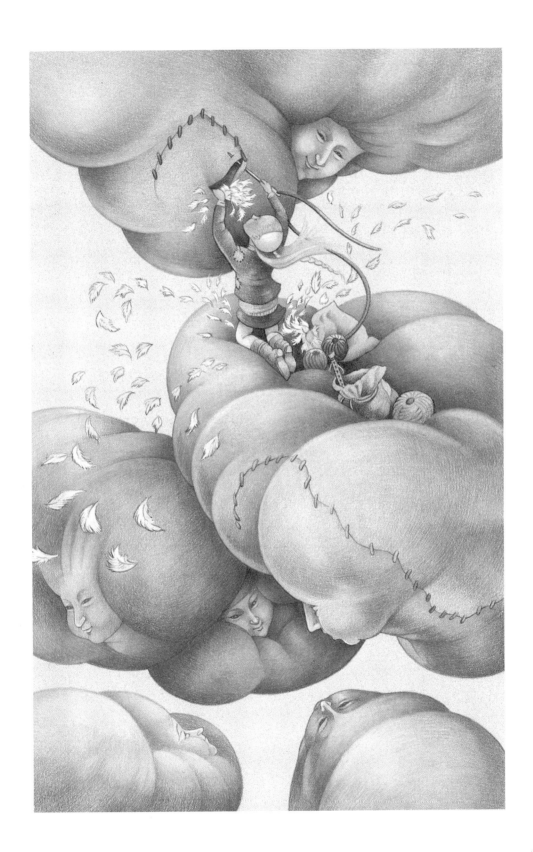

N and on they floated, through the gray chill, until they reached Florida. There they found Mother Nature sunbathing on the beach. "Please come back, Mother Nature," pleaded Sue. "The kingdom's in a terrible mess. It can't do without you."

"No way," she replied. "I won't come back until that kingdom is all cleaned up. I won't return until everything is spick and span."

 UE returned home and told everyone what Mother Nature had said. The townspeople set to work immediately. The kingdom had never seen such hustle and bustle.

They polished, they cleaned, they swept, they scrubbed. They mopped, they wiped, they dusted, and they rubbed. Soon the air, and the water, and the soil were all as clean as a whistle. "Hooray," cheered the people. And they all sat down to wait.

CROSS the meadow came Mother Nature, prancing and dancing with spring right behind her.

The people of the kingdom cheered, but Mother Nature held up her hand to quiet them. "I'll only stay if you promise to keep our kingdom clean," she said. For a brief moment there was silence, and then everyone shouted at once. "We promise, we promise!"

HE king took off his crown and held it out to Sue. "You've saved us," he said. "Now the kingdom is yours."

Sue looked the king right in the eye. "No thank you, Your Majesty," she replied, ever so politely. "I've thought it over and I've decided that I like what I have."

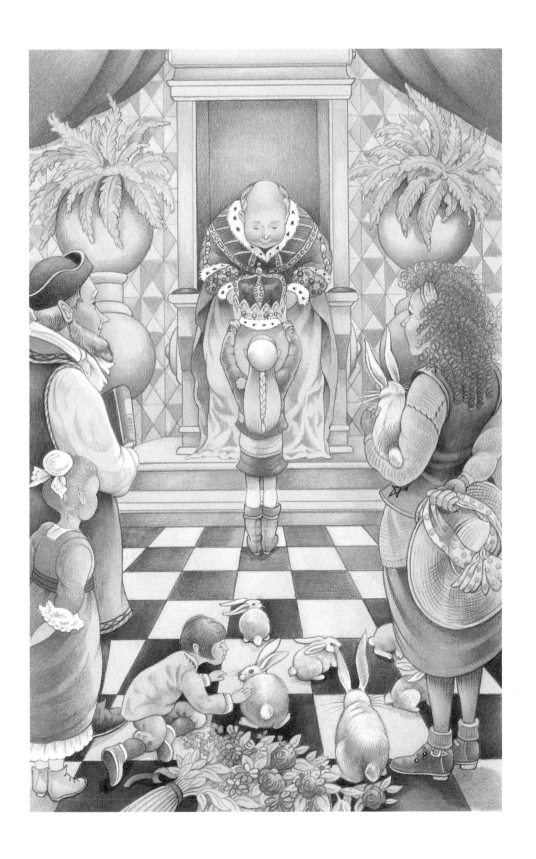

O Sue returned to her cottage and the king to his castle. The townspeople all kept their promise, and from that day forth, Mother Nature and all in her kingdom lived together in peace and harmony.

DATE DUE		
NOV 6 '95		

BAILEY: Lydia
Mother Nature Takes a
Vacation